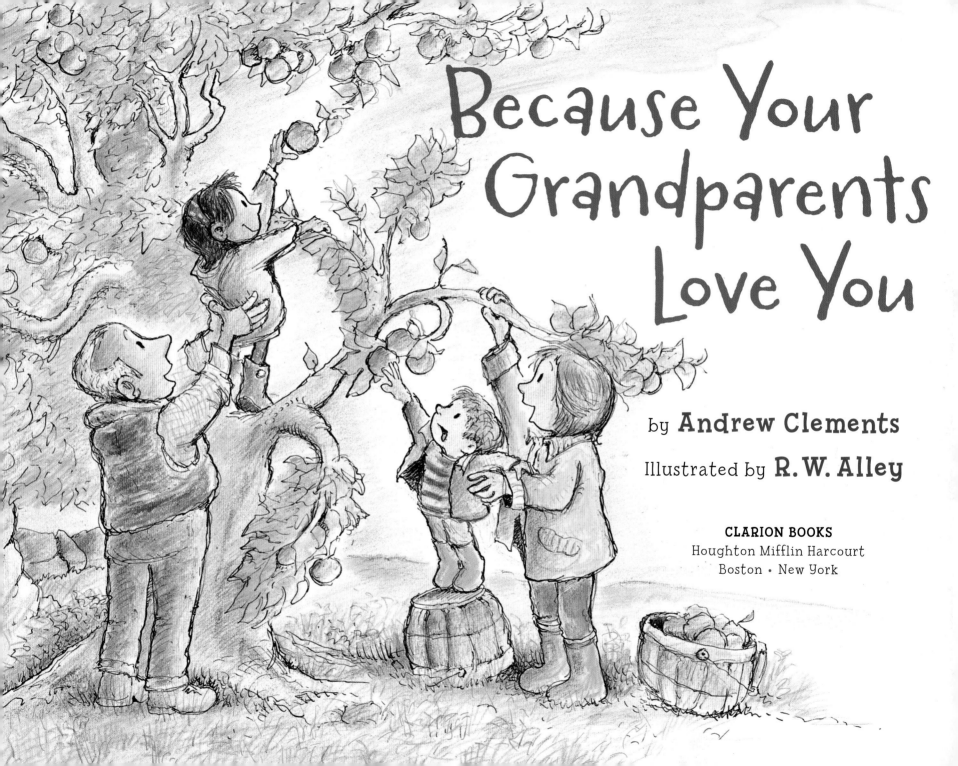

Because Your Grandparents Love You

by **Andrew Clements**

Illustrated by **R. W. Alley**

CLARION BOOKS
Houghton Mifflin Harcourt
Boston • New York

Clarion Books
215 Park Avenue South
New York, New York 10003

Text copyright © 2015 by Andrew Clements
Illustrations copyright © 2015 by R. W. Alley

Clarion Books is an imprint of Houghton Mifflin Harcourt Publishing Company.

www.hmhco.com

The illustrations in this book were executed in pen and ink with
colored pencils, gouache, and crayons on Bristol board.
The text was set in 19-point Billy Serif.

Library of Congress Cataloging-in-Publication Data
Clements, Andrew, 1949-
Because your grandparents love you / Andrew Clements ; illustrated by R. W. Alley.
pages cm
Summary: "Grandparents are the reassuring heroes in this story about a boy and girl who go
on an overnight visit at their grandmother and grandfather's farm."—Provided by publisher.
ISBN 978-0-544-14854-3 (hardcover)
[1. Grandparents—Fiction. 2. Farm life—Fiction.] I. Alley, R. W., 1955- illustrator. II. Title.
PZ7.C59118Bek 2015
[E]—dc23
2014021776

Manufactured in China
SCP 10 9 8 7 6 5 4 3 2 1
4500528653

For Ric and Julie Pierpont, dear
family and devoted grandparents —A.C.

For Bob and Norma,
true grandparents —R.W.A.

WHEN you run into the pasture and step right into a big cowpie, and you yell

GRANDMA!

your grandmother could say,
I'm pretty sure I told you
we have to watch
where we walk around here!

7

But she doesn't.

She gets the hose and sprays
off your shoes.
You put them on the fence to dry,

and then go back inside
for some clean socks . . .
and your boots!

When the horse puts his nose
right against yours
and you stand as still as a statue,

Grampa?

your grandfather
could say,

Well, don't be a scaredy cat!

11

But he doesn't.

Grampa takes a carrot
out of his pocket
and shows you how
to hold it just so.
Then old Jasper
eats it in one bite,
right off of
your hand.

When you want to help feed the cow but can't lift the hay,
your grandmother could say,

Hold on there—that's way too much!

But she doesn't.

Grandma hands you the clippers,
and you cut the string.

And after you put just enough hay into the manger,
the cow swishes her tail and munches her lunch.

When you want
to pick the best apples

but the pole isn't long enough,
your grandfather could say,
*Those lower ones will probably taste
just as good.*

But he doesn't.

He lifts you onto his shoulders
and stands in just the right place.
And then you pick nine of the reddest
apples on the tree.

When you can't get the
hen to move
and she starts to peck
at your hand,
your grandmother could say,
Oh, dear!
It looks like you've gotten her
all upset.

But she doesn't.

She reminds you to talk softly,
and put one hand over each wing,
and gently lift the hen off her nest.
And then there are three fresh eggs
for your basket.

When you turn the peeler in the kitchen
and the whole apple breaks apart,
your grandfather could say,
No, no—you're doing that all wrong.

But he doesn't.

He gets a fresh apple
and helps you turn the crank—
slow and steady, around and around—

and the peel comes
zipping off in one long piece.
In no time at all,
the apples are ready
to go into a pie.

When you help with the fire after dinner
and smoke comes billowing out,
your grandmother
could say,
*Looks like somebody
doesn't know green
wood from dry wood!*

But she doesn't.

She shows you how to open
the damper wider,
and push the wood back farther,
and use plenty of kindling.
And soon the room
is toasty warm.

When you're ready for bed,
and the guest room
seems chilly
and dark and far away,
your grandmother
and grandfather
follow you
up the stairs.

Grampa reads you a story, and when it's over, he clicks off the light. But he turns on the night-light, and Grandma promises to sit in the rocking chair until you're sound asleep.

And after they tuck in your quilt they could say,

All the chickens are nesting now,

or

The moon is shining on the apple tree,

or

Old Jasper will want another carrot tomorrow.

And they do.

And then they say,